Treacle Walker

ALSO BY ALAN GARNER

FICTION

The Weirdstone of Brisingamen

The Moon of Gomrath

Elidor

The Owl Service

Red Shift

A Bag of Moonshine

The Lad of the Gad

The Stone Book Quartet

Strandloper

Thursbitch

Boneland

ESSAYS

The Voice that Thunders

MEMOIR

Where Shall We Run To?

Treacle Walker

Alan Garner

4th ESTATE • *London*

4th Estate
An imprint of HarperCollins*Publishers*
1 London Bridge Street
London SE1 9GF

www.4thEstate.co.uk

HarperCollins*Publishers*
1st Floor, Watermarque Building, Ringsend Road
Dublin 4, Ireland

First published in Great Britain in 2021 by 4th Estate

2

Edited by Robert Lacey

A catalogue record for this book is
available from the British Library

ISBN 978-0-00-847779-0

Set in Adobe Garamond Pro

Printed and bound in the UK using 100% Renewable Electricity at
CPI Group (UK) Ltd

MIX
Paper from
responsible sources
FSC™ C007454

This book is produced from independently certified FSC™ paper
to ensure responsible forest management.

For more information visit: www.harpercollins.co.uk/green

For MGS

Il tempo è ignoranza

Time is ignorance

Carlo Rovelli, *L'ordine del tempo*

I

'Ragbone! Ragbone! Any rags! Pots for rags! Donkey stone!'

Joe looked up from his comic and lifted his eye patch. Noony rattled past the house and the smoke from her engine blew across the yard. It was midday. The sky shone.

'Ragbone! Ragbone! Any rags! Pots for rags! Donkey stone!'

Quick, Joe. Now, Joe.

Joe pulled the patch down, got off his mattress on the top of the chimney cupboard and stood at the big window.

The last of Noony's smoke curled through the valley and along the brook. He could see no one in Barn Croft or Pool Field or Big Meadow or on the track between the top and bottom gates; and trees hid the way up from there to the heath. He went back to bed.

'Ragbone! Ragbone! Any rags! Pots for rags! Donkey stone!'

The voice was below the window. He climbed down again.

There was a white pony in the yard. It was harnessed to a cart, a flat cart, with a wooden chest on it. A man was sitting at a front corner of the cart, holding the reins. His face was creased. He wore a long coat and a floppy high-crowned hat, with hair straggling beneath, and a leather bag was slung from his shoulder across his hip.

'Ragbone! Ragbone! Any rags! Pots for rags! Donkey stone!' He looked up at Joe.

Joe opened the window. Even from there he saw the eyes. They were green violet.

'What do you want?' he said.

'Rag and bone,' said the man. 'And you shall have pot and stone. That's fair. Or isn't it?'

'Wait on,' said Joe. 'I'm coming.' He rummaged in the cupboard and found an old pair of pyjamas. He ran downstairs to his museum and raised the glass lid. There was his collection of birds' eggs and a lamb's shoulder blade he had picked from a mole hill by the railway embankment. He took the shoulder blade, opened the door and went into the yard.

'I've got these.'

'Come aboard, buccaneer,' said the man.

Joe put his foot on a wheel spoke and climbed onto the cart. The man made room for him at the corner, and Joe sat down. He turned his face away.

'What is wrong?' said the man.

'You smell.'

'Not I, Joseph Coppock,' said the man. 'You smell that I stink. Let words be nice.'

'How do you know my name?' said Joe.

'"More know Tom Fool than Tom Fool knows,"' said the man. 'Or don't they?'

Joe jumped from the cart.

'Cob you! Cob you, then!'

'Master Coppock. Come up.'

Joe climbed back, but sat further along the cart.

'What have you brought to market?' The man took the pyjamas. 'These are yours? Your own? You have worn them?'

'They've got holes in.'

The man put the pyjamas to his face and sniffed.

'They've not been washed,' said Joe.

'And what bone?'

'I found this down the banking, near the brook. It's a lamb.'

'Well cleaned, scapulimancer.'

'Are you daft?' said Joe.

'"As Dick's hatband", as they used to say. Open the chest. And choose.'

Joe got up and went to the chest. He lifted the lid.

'Heck!'

The chest was full. Bedded in layers of silk, there were cups, saucers, platters, jugs, big and small: coloured, plain, simple, silvered, gilded, twisted; scenes of dancing, scenes of killing; ships, oceans, seas; beasts, birds, fishes, whales, monsters, houses, castles, mansions, halls; cherubs, satyrs, nymphs; mountains, rivers, forests, lakes, fields and clouds and skies.

'Choose,' said the man. 'One.'

'They're worth loads, this lot,' said Joe.

'Choose.'

'More than jamas and bones.'

'Choose.'

Joe took out every piece and laid them on the cart.

'This,' said Joe.

'That is the least,' said the man.

'It's the best.'

Joe held a round jar no bigger than his hand.

'It is small,' said the man.

'I don't care.'

'Of little price.'

'I don't care. It's grand. Grand as owt.'

The jar was white, glazed, and chipped. Under the rim was painted in blue: 'Poor Mans Friend', and beneath, 'price 1/1½'. On the other side was: 'Prepared only by Beach & Barnicott, SUCCESSORS TO THE LATE Dr. Roberts, Bridport.'

'It's old,' said Joe.

'As some would reckon. Now you shall have donkey stone.'

The man put everything back in the chest and closed the lid. There was an oval brass plate in the middle of the lid, and on it Joe saw a name engraved in flowing letters.

'Blinking heck!'

'What is wrong?' said the man.

'My name! That's my name! My own name! There! And Real Writing! See at it!'

'At this time all is yours. You have chosen. Next, you must have this.'

'Blinking heck.'

The man opened his bag and took something out. 'Here.' It was a stone, rough and grey, the size and shape of a bar of soap.

'Blinking heck.'

He put the stone into Joe's hand. One side was plain; on the other, along the whole length, was cut the outline of a horse, legs and tail outstretched, head forward, thin.

'We are equal. The trade is done.'

'And what am I supposed to do with this effort?' said Joe.

'Use it.'

'How?'

'As you have need.'

'You're twitting me,' said Joe. 'I'm going in. I mustn't catch the sun.'

'You would be swift to outrun that one,' said the man. 'The craven nidget who flees the dark and will not come back till morning.'

'I've been poorly,' said Joe.

'Then I shall bid you good day; but have shade here under your pear. Heat and old meat don't marry. And the leaves of pear are cold, its virtues earthy.'

'You can come inside, if you want,' said Joe. 'It's cooler.'

'Since I may.'

'Suit yourself. I'm not bothered,' said Joe.

He went into the house. The man followed, but paused and looked at the step as he crossed the threshold.

The house was three rooms parted by timber-framed walls and joined by open doorways. A round iron fire basket was in the base of the chimney, which was a room of itself, made of the same timbers, walked through from two opposite sides.

Joe and the man went into the chimney and sat on the oak sill of the base, facing each other across cold ashes. Joe put the pot and the stone next to him on the sill. The man took his bag from his shoulder and set it on the floor.

'Why the patch, buccaneer?' said the man.

'I've got Lazy Eye,' said Joe. 'I must wear the patch over the good one so the other will catch up. But it's not doing owt. It gives me headaches. And I can't see proper.'

'"What the eye doesn't see,"' said the man, '"the heart doesn't grieve for." Or does it?'

'It's a flipping nuisance,' said Joe. 'Eh, but my name … And Real Writing.'

'Patience, my amblyopic friend. Patience.'

'Oh ha ha ha. Hee hee hee. Elephant's eggs in a rhubarb tree.'

The man sat and did not speak. Everything about him was poor. His shoes were hard leather and too big and were fastened with a strap, and there were open splits across the tops, as if they had been slashed. He wore no socks.

Joe shifted to the side, and back. 'Your face,' he said. 'One road, it's old. The other, it's not. Straight, it's all sorts. Same as them knacky postcards change when you look. It's this blooming eye.'

'Wellaway.' The man gazed into the tapering stack above.

'Who are you?' said Joe.

'Who? What?' said the man. 'Is there a difference?'

'Can you not talk sense? What's your name?'

Outside, the iron ring handle of the door banged on the wood three slow times, sounding through the house.

Joe went to the small window by the door and looked. He saw no one. Only the pony under the tree; and the bleach of heat.

'There's nobody there,' he said.

'Then no body wishes to come in,' said the man.

Bang. Bang. Bang.

Joe felt the door shake.

'What must I do?' he said.

Bang. Bang. Bang.

Joe looked again. The pony. The tree. The heat.

He lifted the latch.

A wind threw the door onto him, shoving him against the stack. And night spilled in. Snow stung his face. He forced the door against the wind and the latch clanged shut. He clung to the chimney post. But night was in the room, a sheet of darkness, flapping from wall to wall. It changed shape, swirling, flowing. It dropped to the ground and ruckled over the floor bricks; then up to the joists and beams of the ceiling; hung, fell, humped. It shrieked, reared against the chimney opening, but did not enter. It surged through the house by cracks and gaps in the timbers, out under the eaves. There was a whispering, silence; and on the floor snow melted to tears.

'My name,' said the man, 'is Treacle Walker.'

II

'Cripes!'

Joe let go of the post. He flung himself against the stench, the sour, into the coat, onto the vile beneath. And the man opened his arms to let him in, but did not hold him.

Joe roared. He yelled. He retched. Then he pushed himself away and crawled to the opposite sill, and sat, his wrists on his knees, shaking; his head drooped.

'It was a hurlothrumbo of winter,' said the man. 'A lomperhomock of night. Nothing more.'

Joe could not speak.

'But summer is nearly come.'

Joe lifted his head. 'Treacle.'

'Treacle.'

'Walker.'

'Treacle Walker I have in this land.'

'What sort of a name is that?'

'I heal.'

'Heal. Make better.'

'All things; save jealousy. Which none can.'

He opened his bag, and took out a bone. It was a shin; narrow; old; hollow; yellow; crazed with black lines; polished; and holes cut in, and a slit at one end.

'What's that?' said Joe.

'I made it from a man that sang.'

'Can I have a see?'

Treacle Walker passed the bone to Joe. He held it and felt its shape.

'What's it for?'

Treacle Walker took back the bone, put his mouth to the slit, his fingers on the holes, closed his eyes, and played. The chimney filled with tune.

It was a tune with wings, trampling things, tightened strings, boggarts and bogles and brags on their feet; the man in the oak, sickness and fever, that set in long, lasting sleep the whole great world with the sweetness of sound the bone did play.

Joe sat and did not speak. The chimney was silent.

'It is the way for him to sing now,' said Treacle Walker.

'Can I have a go?'

Treacle Walker passed the bone across the fire basket.

'What must I do?'

'Hold. And breathe.'

Joe put the bone to his lips. 'Like this?' He blew. The notes came, pure; the call of a cuckoo.

Across the valley, a cuckoo answered.

'Did you hear that? Cuckoo!'

'Unfound bones sing louder. Draw a pail of water.'

'You what?' said Joe.

'Draw a pail of water.' Treacle Walker held out his hand for the bone.

'You're daft. You are. Daft.'

'Joseph Coppock. Draw the pail.'

'That's you. Daft. Right enough.' But Joe went out to the well and pumped a bucket of water. He came back and banged it down. 'You and your hurlolomperjobs. I near cacked me.'

'Stone the step,' said Treacle Walker.

'How do you mean, "stone"?'

'Put the donkey stone to the water, then rub the step.'

'All of it?'

'All.'

'Why?'

'To keep the house.'

'I don't get you,' said Joe.

'Do it.'

'Show me.'

'Not I. The stone is yours,' said Treacle Walker.

'Oh, ta very much I'm sure.'

Joe opened the door, and knelt. The stone fitted his hand, the horse against his palm, and he dipped it in the water.

'Eh up!'

'What is it?' said Treacle Walker from inside the chimney.

'My name again! On the stone! Silver! Letters! At the side. All round! My name!'

'The stone is for you. You are for the stone.'

'They've gone. I can't see them.'

'And why should you, once you know?'

'But they were there.'

'Do it.'

'They were. You're daft. Like I said.'

'Do it.'

'Daft as a brush.'

Joe rubbed the donkey stone on the step. The grey left a white mark. He dipped and rubbed, dipped and rubbed, until the step was all over white and shining.

'Is it done?' said Treacle Walker.

'Yes.'

Treacle Walker came from the chimney and looked at the step.

'Keep it so.'

'Why?'

'"Every why has its wherefore." Or hasn't it?'

'Get away with your bother,' said Joe.

Treacle Walker looked out across the valley.

'"Iram, biram, brendon, bo,
Where did all the children go?
They went to the east. They went to the west.
They went where the cuckoo has its nest."'

He looked down.

'Such tarradiddles, Joseph Coppock. Such macaronics. Such nominies for a young head. And if I had been young? If. If I had been. If I had.'

III

Joe pushed himself up on the mattress. 'Treacle Walker!'

Noony rattled past the house and the smoke from her engine blew across the yard. The sky shone.

He climbed down to the floor and stood at the window.

The last of Noony's smoke curled through the valley and along the brook. He could see no one in Barn Croft or Pool Field or Big Meadow or on the track between the top and bottom gates; and trees hid the way up from there to the heath.

He went downstairs and opened the door. The step gleamed white.

'Treacle Walker!'

Joe went to his museum. There was his egg collection, but no lamb's shoulder blade. Instead there was a grey stone, and next to it a round jar no bigger than his hand. The jar was white, glazed, and chipped. Under the rim was painted in blue: 'Poor Mans Friend', and beneath, 'price 1/1½'. On the other side was: 'Prepared only by Beach & Barnicott, SUCCESSORS TO THE LATE Dr. Roberts, Bridport.'

IV

Joe lifted the jar out.

It was clean, but the chips had dirt in them, as if the jar had been in the earth. There were traces of green violet paste inside on the base. He wiped off the dirt with his handkerchief and spit and rubbed the paste with his finger. The paste was sticky and marked his skin. He smelt it. The smell was warm and harsh. He put the jar back in the museum.

He picked up the stone. The cut horse stretched along the whole length. The line of the body, tail and legs was made of five curves; the head square, the eye a dot, the ears two spikes, the muzzle an open beak.

He turned the stone over.

There was nothing on the other side; just the plain, rough surface. Joe looked closer. He went to the door and the light. The step glistened, still wet from the whitening; but the stone was grey, unmarked, unworn, and dry.

Down the field a cuckoo called. It was near: in a copse of alder bog by the brook.

Joe put the stone in his pocket and ran across the yard to the gate for a better view over Big Meadow down to the brook. The cuckoo called again, from the edge of the copse. He looked, but the leaves were thick and were blurred by his eye. He lifted his patch to see better. Nothing. The bog was silent.

The sun was on his neck, and he began to feel dizzy. He had been out too long, and should not have run. Light glared, and he pulled the patch down. The elastic slipped and he moved it and wiped the sweat from below the band. His finger touched his eyelid, and jagged light and pain filled his head.

Joe zigzagged back to the house, covering half his face with his hands. He fell onto a wooden settle, pressing his head against a cushion, but the pain and the light still flashed, making him cry out.

Then light and pain were gone. Joe pulled up the patch and opened both eyes. He went upstairs to the long mirror in his bedroom and looked. There was nothing wrong; only a smudge of green violet where his stained finger had touched the lid of the good eye. He still felt dizzy from the heat and the sunlight, and he went back and lay on the settle, as he always did when he had a bilious sick headache.

V

'Come in, Joe,' the man said.

Joe went into the room and sat on the chair.

'How are things?'

'All right.'

'Let's have a shufti, then.' He pulled his chair up. 'Let's do the business.' He switched off the room lamp and pushed his face against Joe's. 'Now look straight ahead.' He shone a bright light into Joe's eye. It hurt. 'Excellent. Now the other. Take your patch off.' The light hurt more. 'Excellent.' He put a metal frame with round eye holes on Joe's nose and lodged it behind his ears. He slotted a blank disc into one of the holes then walked himself across the floor on the wheels of his chair to a screen at the other side of the room. A white dot and a red line appeared. 'The usual drill. Keep your eye on the dot.

Is the line to the right or the left, or through the middle?'

'The middle.'

'Excellent.' He turned the image. 'Is the line above or below, or through the middle?'

'The middle.'

'Excellent.' He moved the blank disc to the other hole. 'Same again, please, Joe.' He flashed lights on and off, changing the disc, asking questions. He switched on the room lamp. 'All tickety-boo. At least we know your eyes point in the same direction.' He moved the disc across.

'Now I want you to look at the chart.' There was a white board with rows of black letters, each row smaller than the one above, hanging on the opposite wall. 'Tell me which is the last line you can read without bother.'

'Number six,' said Joe. 'E, D, F, C, Z, P.'

'Excellent.'

'I can do the next.'

'Surprise me.'

'F. E. L. O. P. Z. – O?'

'Nearly.' He moved the disc so that Joe was using his good eye. 'And which is the last line you can read now without bother?'

'The bottom,' said Joe.

'The bottom?'

'Yes. A, B, E, D, O, C, T, I, S.'

'What?'

'A, B, E, D, O, C, T, I, S.'

'And the rest?'

'Dead easy. Top line, H. Next, I, C. Next, L, A, P. Then I, S, E, X. Then I, L, I, S, E. Then X, T, A, T, P, R. Then E, T, I, O, Q, V, O. Then Q, V, E, V, I, L, I, S. Then S, P, E, R, N, I, T, V. Then R, A, S, T, V, L, T, I, S, A. Then M, A, T, V, R, P, L, V, S. And A, B, E, D, O, C, T, I, S.'

'Not funny, old son.'

'What isn't?'

'It doesn't help if you faff around.'

'I'm not faffing.'

'Hmm.' He changed the disc over. 'Press on regardless. How far can you read now?'

'E, D, F, C, Z, P. It's the wonky eye.'

He took the frame off Joe's nose. 'And how do you see with both together?'

'Squiffy.'

'Hmm.'

'What's up?' said Joe.

'The letters you read with your good eye aren't there.'

'Yes they are! You swapped the board!'

'I didn't.' He set the frame back on Joe's nose and gave him a sheet of paper and a pencil. 'Put the patch over your weak eye and write down what you see with the other.'

'Don't want to.'

'Come on. There's a good lad.'

'Where?'

'Come on. Just for me.'

'It's daft.' Joe worked the patch under the frame and wrote.

'Thanks, Joe.' He took the paper. 'Interesting. Very, very interesting.'

'What is? What's up?'

'You tell me, my old mucker,' he said, and gave the paper back to Joe. 'You tell me.'

Joe got off the chair and went close to the chart. He read it, then moved his patch over and read again.

'Heck.'

'Yes?'

'It looks different,' said Joe. 'Like there's two of 'em.'

'But there aren't. There's only one chart.'

'What's wrong? What's wrong with my eyes?'

'There's not a lot wrong with your eyes, Joe. What beats me is your sight.'

VI

Joe got off the settle and sat in the chimney. The sick headache had cleared. He took the paper out of his pocket, and spread it on his knee and read what he had written.

H
IC
LAP
ISEX
ILISE
XTATPR
ETIOQVO
QVEVILIS
SPERNITV
RASTVLTISA
MATVRPLVS
ABEDOCTIS

What the dickens?

Outside the door, close by, a cuckoo called. Joe stuffed the paper back and opened the door. Nothing.

'Where are you?'

A call came from the alders.

'Wait your sweat!'

Joe put his wellies on. He took his catapult and went into the yard, picked up small pebbles and dropped them in his pockets. He went through the gate and down Big Meadow, climbed over the earth bank that bordered the trees and onto the bog, catapult at the ready.

The copse was old and had long not been worked. The stems from the root stools had grown to full trunks, making islands of clumps with the roots running and twining among dead leaves, and black water beneath. Where light came through there were thickets of undergrowth: nettles, brambles and whatever else could live.

He put his catapult in his pocket and moved from stool to stool, feeling for roots to stand on. If he slipped, his leg sank in deeper than his wellies and he had to grab and pull himself out against the suck.

'Where are you?'

The cuckoo called to his front. He went on into the bog.

The bog dragged at him. Soon he had to stop and rest against a tree. Mosquitoes whined and bit. The only sounds were the wings of insects. The air was heavy with marsh smells. There was no wind, and what sky there was showed all one bronze.

The cuckoo called to his left. He turned. It called to his right. He splashed towards it. Now it was behind. Joe braced himself between two trunks to get his breath.

'Give over messing!'

The cuckoo answered from another side. Then another. It was all around him. And another. Another. Another. Another. Another. 'Give over!' Another.

'Right, then! If that's the game, I'm out! No barleys!'

Joe looked for his tracks to go back, but there were none; only the black water, the red veins of root, the dead leaves and mire. The sky was no guide. He moved his patch to use his good eye in the gloom. The alders stood so close he could not see the fields; but the copse was small, and if he walked straight he would come to the earth bank or find the brook and follow that. Joe set off, keeping to each tree in front for his line.

And the cuckoo was all about him, in the air, in his ears, in his lungs, in his head.

His bones hurt from the pull of the mud, and his hands stung on the roots and lost their feeling so that they did not grip. His wellies were full and heavy with water. But he went on.

He went on. He went till he could not go. He put his arms round a trunk. Everywhere was the same. He had walked straight, he knew. The copse was not big. But however he moved there was nothing beyond: no bank, no brook, no field, no end; only cuckoo, wet, and slutch.

He fell on the alder stool. 'Help!'

A man sat up in the bog. 'Why the stramash, Joseph Coppock,' he said, 'and you with the stone in your pocket?'

He wore a close hood made of leather, tied under his chin. The rest of him was bare. Hood and skin and eyes were all the same copper brown.

Joe lay across the stool, held between the trunks.

'May a body not rest in his bog?' said the man.

'Can't …'

'"Can't never did."'

'… get.'

'Is that it? Is that the hue and the cry you woke me for?'

'No … way. All … over. Same.'

'Move the dish clout and shut your glims.'

'Damn …'

'Do it.'

'Bloody …'

'Do it.'

Joe lifted his patch to his forehead and shut his eyes.

'Are you seeing me?'

'Bloody damn …'

'Open a glim.'

'Piss off …' He opened his good eye.

'Are you seeing me?'

'Piss off!'

'Off or on are one to me. Shut that glim and open the other. Do it.'

Joe grabbed a trunk. 'Where are you? Where've you gone?'

He opened his good eye again. The man was there and had not moved.

The bog spun. 'Where were you?'

'Where I am, Joseph Coppock,' said the man. 'And where were you?'

Joe shut his good eye and looked with the other. He could not see the man. He changed over. The man was there. He changed again. He changed back. And changed again. It was always the same. His good eye saw the man; his weak eye saw only the bog. With both eyes open he saw, but not as clearly in the blur.

'Are we going to be at peep-bo till night?' said the

man. 'Or shall we be getting you out of here and me to me dreamings?'

'What's up with my eyes?'

'You have the glamourie,' said the man. 'In just the one. And that's no bad thing, if you have the knowing. She'll be the governor while you learn the hang of it, and when you've got that you'll be fine as filliloo. But you need the both of them. What sees is seen.'

The man stood. Water and leaves dripped from him.

'Shut the glamourie and turn about. And when you've looked, open her again.'

Joe twisted his head round and closed his good eye. He saw the green of Big Meadow between the trees, and above it the house. The copse was small, and the bank near. He opened the good eye. The bog was everywhere.

'And that's the way to do it,' said the man.

Joe kept his good eye shut, and worked himself upright. He left the alder stool and trod across to the bank and over into Big Meadow. He opened his eye and looked back. The man was standing behind him.

'Use the two glims together,' he said, 'till we get you home. And after, don't wear your clout. For though at the first you'll be in a flustication with it all, you'll be needing the both. I've tellt you. What sees is seen.'

'Come with us,' said Joe. 'I don't feel right.'

'I'll not,' said the man. 'I must have me bog and me trees, else I'll be drying out, and that won't do. The sweet smiling of a step will hold you safe. But we can sit here on the bank till you're fit to go; and you can tell me why you were clanjandering in me bog at all.'

'I wanted to see the cuckoo.'

'Why heed cuckoo?'

'I want to see it,' said Joe. 'It comes every year. But I've never seen. Only heard.'

'Well, well.'

'What's that mean?'

'Well, well.'

'Anyroad, I collect birds' eggs. I've got ever so many; all sorts.'

'How?' said the man. 'An egg got is an egg gone.'

'I'm not with you.'

'Why, it's eaten.'

'You don't eat them,' said Joe. 'You make a hole at either end with your knife and blow them. Then you put the shells in the case.'

'For what?' said the man.

'So you can see at them.'

'Why?'

'To learn you. About birds.'

'They do? And how are you to get cuckoo's egg?'

'You listen. Then when you hear it you follow it and pop it with your catapult and get the egg. But only one. You leave the rest.'

'For cuckoo?'

'Yes. If you took them all it wouldn't be fair.'

'Oh, you're the very know-all of cuckoo!' said the man. 'You have the book of him!'

'What's so funny?' said Joe.

'I'm laughing for the joy of meeting such a high-learnt cuckoo young-feller-me-lad as yourself.'

'I've been at it a while,' said Joe. 'That's why. But I haven't got a cuckoo yet.'

'And I wish you the luck on it there,' said the man. 'So I do. But you're the delight of the ages to me; for there's little laughing in a bog. And less in dreaming.'

'Why've you got no clothes on?' said Joe.

'And wouldn't they be drenched, if I had?' said the man.

'What's the hat for, then?'

'Against the rain.'

'Who are you?' said Joe.

'Thin Amren is the name. And that's enough. I'm not the one to be out of the water. I need me wetness. Now think on what I've tellt you. And to show the meaning, put the clout to the glamourie and use the glim that's in the mirligoes.'

Joe moved his patch down. 'What's mirlithingies?' he said.

The man was not to be seen.

Joe ran.

VII

It was a blue-grey day; no use to anyone. Joe lay on his mattress reading his Knockout and playing marbles against himself on the top of the cupboard. Sometimes he let the other Joe win, but he never let him take his dobber glass alley. Inside the glass were twists and fiery swirls of all colours. It was his biggest marble, and it had just beaten a blood alley. The blood alley was good. It was made of red and white glass, but Joe couldn't see into it like he could the dobber.

Knockout was the best comic, better than The Beano or The Dandy, because it had daft ideas. And the best in it was Stonehenge Kit the Ancient Brit, who was always fighting Whizzy the Wicked Wizard and his chums the Brit Bashers. Whizzy wore a pointed hat.

This time, Kit was falling out of a tree, and he dropped thump woof bam crash on Whizzy, who was having forty-one winks in a hammock, which is a lot of holes tied with string, and Kit bundled him up in the hammock to take him as a prisoner for King Kongo and swap him for two cigarette-cards. He met a Brit Basher disguised as a milk maid. The Brit Basher was wearing a wig and carrying a big jar on his shoulder. Kit asked him the way to the palace, but the Brit Basher said **TRY THIS WAY, MATEY!** and dropped the jar over Kit, and then he set Whizzy free from the hammock. What would happen to our hero now?

Joe was so excited he put the dobber in his mouth and sucked it like a gobstopper.

The Brit Basher picked up a boulder and Whizzy said he was going to lift the jar, and the Brit Basher must plonk the boulder on Kit's head. But when Whizzy did lift the jar there was only a round hole in the ground. Kit had been standing on the cover; and in the next picture he was sliding down a pole in a shaft, and there was a sign saying **TO THE STONEHENGE UNDERGROUND RAILWAY**.

Joe laughed; and Kit looked up and winked at him and put a hand out and got hold of the frame of the picture to stop himself. The line sank under the weight of his grip; and the other three sides opened to keep the square.

Kit let go of the pole and pressed the side of the picture to make it bigger. He pulled himself through onto the mattress. **HOW DO, JOE?** he said. The words came out of his mouth in a bubble, just as they did in the comic, and made no sound. He jumped down from the cupboard. Joe heard the clump of his feet. He sat up and saw Kit's back reflected in the long mirror. In the mirror Kit was running towards the door next to the chimney. But in the room there was no one.

Joe felt a draught of cold air. He turned to the picture. He touched the square with his finger. His finger went in as if there was no paper, and his hand was on rock. He reached and held the pole. He twisted against the rock and saw a circle of daylight above, and the dark of two heads, one with a pointed hat.

Joe glanced under his arm into the room. The wall and chimney were at a slant. He felt the pole quiver in his hand. He looked up again. Two shapes were sliding down the pole towards him. He shouted, and the dobber glass alley fell from his mouth into the shaft. He heard it hitting the sides. The sound grew fainter, but he did not hear it hit the bottom. He jerked back onto his mattress, and a man with a pointed hat was on the pole and holding the frame. He hopped onto the cupboard. It was Whizzy and behind him came a Brit Basher. ***WOT ABOUT THIS ONE, GUV?*** he said. Whizzy said ***NAH. WE'LL COME BACK LATER AND BIFF HIM FOR THAT BRICK AND POT HE'S GOT.*** They jumped down into the room, and Joe saw their backs in the mirror as they disappeared through the reflection of the doorway by the chimney.

Joe lay on the mattress until the room was steady. He took his patch from his pocket and pulled it over his eye. The picture shrank to the page; and Kit was on the pole, a drawing in the comic, not looking at him. Joe put his finger out, and felt paper. There was sand on his shirt from the rock.

VIII

he got down from [illegible] the [illegible]

[illegible] saw Ba[illegible] and [illegible]

[illegible]

from [illegible] side [illegible]

room. He looked away from the [illegible]

door by the [illegible]

the [illegible]

and [illegible]

[illegible]

[illegible]

marbles. They were all there, except for the [illegible] glass alley he [illegible]. He went to the window to look closely at [illegible] light.

The [illegible] and [illegible] Walker [illegible] against the [illegible]

Joe got down from the cupboard and went to the mirror. He saw himself and the room behind. He touched the hard glass. He pushed it. He moved from side to side, so that he saw into the whole room. He backed away from the mirror towards the door by the chimney, watching. When he reached the door he turned and looked over his shoulder, and saw himself looking over his shoulder in the doorway, nothing like Kit and Whizzy and the Brit Basher in the mirror running from the empty room.

He went back up to his mattress and counted his marbles. They were all there, except for the dobber glass alley. He shook his comic, but nothing fell out. He went to the window to look closely in the better light.

The pony and cart were in the yard; and Treacle Walker was sitting against the pear tree.

Joe ran down and opened the door. The clouds had broken.

'Treacle Walker!'

He ran across the yard into the sun.

'Joseph Coppock.'

'What are you at? Where've you been?'

'I have been through Hickety, Pickety, France and High Spain, by crinkum-crankums, crooks and straights,' said Treacle Walker. 'And I am at your pear, with my ears in my hat, my back in my coat, and two squat kickering tattery shoes full of road-wayish water. The sun is not good for you, as I recall.'

'So what?'

'Your visage is wan. If we may, let us go to the chimney and calm our thought.'

'Why?'

'You are a trifle furibund.'

'Shurrup.'

They went to the house. Treacle Walker paused at the step. 'May I enter?'

'It's up to you,' said Joe.

'It is not up to me,' said Treacle Walker. 'Now that the stoning is done, neither I nor any other can cross save by your leave. May I enter?'

'Have it your own way,' said Joe. 'You can come in if you like. It's daft.'

They went in and sat facing each other across the fire basket in the chimney.

'What is amiss, Joseph Coppock?' said Treacle Walker.

'What's amiss?' said Joe. 'I'll tell you what's amiss. I shall. I shall that. You come here, you and your box and your pots and your donkey stone, and fetch in enough to make me frit to death. You're on about bones and all sorts; and then you're off, some road or other, and I can't tell where I am. I've got a pain in my eye. I can't see proper. And I go down the bog and get stuck; and this chap with no clothes on and a daft silly hat, he sits up in the water and he makes no more sense than you do. He says I've got glam-meritis, and then Stonehenge Kit, he's gone, and so's my best dobber; and Whizzy's with a Brit Basher and they're after Kit and the mirror's all wrong then he's back in the picture. And there's this here.' Joe pulled the crumpled paper from his pocket and lobbed it across the fire basket. 'What's happening? What the heck's up?'

Treacle Walker straightened the paper and looked at it.

'Did you write this, Joseph Coppock?'

'I was having my eyes tested –'

'When?'

'When they were being tested. And the man said –'

'What man?'

'The man in the room.'

'Which room?'

'Where I was having my eyes tested!'

'Where was the room?' said Treacle Walker.

'It was – there,' said Joe.

'Who was the man?'

'The man testing my eyes! Give over!'

'I am but asking the question,' said Treacle Walker. 'Who was the man?'

'He was – I dunno. He said what I read wasn't real. So I wrote it, but it still wasn't real, he said.'

'Yet it is,' said Treacle Walker. 'And how does it speak to you?'

'It's jumbled letters, same as they always are, but not like he said.'

'Jumbled letters? "Hic lapis exilis extat pretio quoque vilis. Spernitur a stultis. Amatur plus ab edoctis." Two catalectic hexameters. You have no Latin?'

'No what?'

'"This stone is small, of little price; spurned by fools, more honoured by the wise." My friend, you saw; yet you do not see.'

Treacle Walker leaned his head against the timber behind him and looked up into the stack.

'Axis mundi.'

'Eh?'

'The chimney. It is the heart of all that is. The sky turns on it. It is the way between.'

'Between what?'

'The earth, the heavens and the sapient stars.'

'It's to let smoke out,' said Joe.

Treacle Walker went to the door.

'May I pass?'

'Don't be daft.'

'Then I presume an affirmative.'

He crossed the step.

'Joseph Coppock. When Thin Amren wakes and cuckoo calls,' he opened his bag and reached inside, 'look to your dobber.' He put the glass alley into Joe's hand and closed the door.

IX

Joe lay on the bank of the brook at the bottom of Big Meadow where there was a smooth piece of water near the bridge. He was watching his reflection. He lifted his hand. He could see that. He put his hand behind his head. The reflection did the same. He held his hand in front of him and peered between his fingers. The reflection did the same. He reached down and put his hand in the water. The reflection broke, and all he saw was his hand and arm in the brook. The water settled. Now he saw his face again.

'And why are we bung-up and squinting like a bag of nails?'

Thin Amren was on the bank opposite, in the shade of an alder.

'What are you doing? What do you want?' said Joe.

'I thought I'd take me a little walk.'

'You said you had to keep wet.'

'And so I must. But there am I in me bog, and I see you here, at the glamourie. And I'm thinking to be with you for a laugh and a crack; for I'm missing you so.'

'I'm plundering about mirrors,' said Joe.

'Well, there are worse ways with a day.' Thin Amren sat and put his feet on the bed of the brook. The water settled. Joe stared.

'Why the gawk of a throttled earwig?' said Thin Amren.

'I can't see your face in the water,' said Joe. 'You're not there.'

'That's because I'm here,' said Thin Amren.

'Why can't I see you?'

'I own no looking-glass.'

'That's daft,' said Joe. 'And another thing. Why live in a bog?'

'And if I didn't,' said Thin Amren, 'should I not rot?'

'And all that dreaming stuff.'

'What else should a body do when he sleeps?'

'How long have you been there?' said Joe. 'In the bog.'

'A honeycomb of ages.'

'How long's that?'

'From then till now. And you?'

'What about me?'

'How long have you been up in the fine chimney house?'

'Always. I live there.'

'And how is "always"?'

'It's – always,' said Joe.

'Well, that's us suited, both,' said Thin Amren. 'You in your chimney. Me in me bog. Snug as a bug in a rug.'

'What's that supposed to mean?'

'Do you see yon whirligig of water there?' Thin Amren pointed to an eddy below an alder root by the bridge. 'He doesn't move. But water, she goes by. Then what's whirligig?'

'I dunno. It just – is,' said Joe.

'Then what is brook?' said Thin Amren.

'It's the brook.'

'And brook was here yesterday,' said Thin Amren. 'And she'll be here tomorrow. Whirligig stays. Though he's not the same water. Then what is yesterday? What today? What tomorrow? Whirligig, what is he? What is brook?'

'Oh, dry up,' said Joe.

'That's the last I'll be doing' said Thin Amren. 'I asked a question. Whirligig neither asks nor cares.'

'You're as bad as he is,' said Joe. 'Treacle Walker. He's daft, too. Do you know him? He says he knows you.'

'Treacle Walker?' said Thin Amren. 'Treacle Walker? Me know that pickthank psychopomp? I know him, so I do. I know him. Him with his pots for rags and his bag and his bone and his doddering nag and nookshotten cart and catchpenny oddments. Treacle Walker? I'd not trust that one's arse with a fart.'

'Well, I like him, anyroad,' said Joe. 'A bit. I think. Yes. I do. I like him a lot. He's daft. I can't get him to talk sense. And he pongs. He pongs; but he makes me laugh. Well, sometimes.'

'And he comes when cuckoo calls.'

'Does he?'

'He does. And what is cuckoo?'

'It's a bird, fathead.'

'A bird,' said Thin Amren. 'Oh, it's you that has the knowing of it.'

'When you hear it, it's nearly summer,' said Joe.

'And beasts are bangled, and barns are bare. And the reiver comes over the hill.'

'Eh?'

'Cuckoo is a two-face bliss,' said Thin Amren. 'A bitter call. And I must get me fat head to me bog and me dreamings. Else, Whirligig, who'll care for him? Now use both your glims. I've tellt you once, and I've tellt you twice, and I'll tell you thrice. What sees is seen. I'll tell you more. What's out is in; what's in is out. Don't wear the clout. There! Aren't I the poet! That's a darling rhyme for a day.'

Thin Amren stood and walked along the bank and into the copse. Joe watched until he could not see; then went up to the house and lay on the settle and counted the joists and beams in the ceiling.

'Whirligig.' 'Cycle pump.' 'Ask this Monday.' 'What sees is seen.' 'What's out is in; what's in is out.' Barmpots. The pair of them.

He got off the settle and climbed the stairs to his bed, picked up a Knockout and began to read.

It was Our Ernie, Mrs. Entwhistle's Little Lad. That was his second favourite. Ernie wore a big cap and had adventures with his chum, a caterpillar called Charlie, who never did anything but watch and say sarky things about what Ernie was doing. Then, in the last picture, Ernie always came home and said **WHAT'S FOR TEA, MA?** And his Pa, who had a big moustache and smoked a pipe upside down, always said **DAFT, I CALL IT**.

Joe turned the page to read Stonehenge Kit the Ancient Brit.

He was looking at his house; his house, with the embankment behind it, and Noony going past; a picture of his own house. At the side was **OO-ER, CHUMS. WHAT'S WHIZZY UP TO NOW? NO**

GOOD, I RECKON. And Whizzy was walking along Big Meadow, with the Brit Basher carrying a club, and he was saying HEH-HEH! CACKLES!

In the next picture they were in the yard, and Whizzy said SPIFLICATE THAT THERE DOOR! And the Brit Basher said GOOD THINKING, GUV. SHEER GENIUS, THAT'S WOT IT IS.

In the next picture, the Brit Basher was standing in front of the door with his club lifted. But in the next the Brit Basher was turning away, and saying COO, GUV. LOOK. STEPS IS STONED. Then in the next it was Whizzy's face, with his pointed hat jumping off his head, and him saying PSHAW! PAH! AND TCHAH! Then he was going round the house and peering in at the windows, but they were small, with mullions that made them too narrow for him to get through. GNASH, GROAN, SNARL, HIDEOUS HOWL AND YAH! said Whizzy.

The last picture was the house by itself at the top of Big Meadow, and someone was looking from the upstairs window. And at the side was WHAT

HAPPENS NEXT, CHUMS? WAIT TILL NEXT WEEK TO FIND OUT!

Joe scrabbled through all his comics, but the Knockout that followed was missing.

X

Bang. Bang. Bang.

Three times the handle on the door.

Joe shot under the blankets and tugged them over his head.

Bang. Bang. Bang.

He reached for his pillow and covered his ears.

Bang. Bang. Bang.

He was sweating. His eyes were shut. All he saw were swirls of purple on the black of his lids. He had no spit; the thud in his ears made the silence worse. He could not slow his breath.

Stillness.

He moved the pillow and pulled the blankets down to his nose and opened his eyes. The sun shone sideways in the window and the sky was bright. He sat up and listened.

Stillness.

Joe climbed down and moved over the floor, not letting the boards creak, to the edge of the window frame and looked out.

The pony and cart were under the pear, and Treacle Walker was on the path by the door, holding the round handle.

'You daft beggar!'

Joe ran down the stairs and opened the door.

'What are you at? Sounding like them lomperwhatsits!'

'How else might one wield the ferrous weight?' said Treacle Walker. 'May one come in?'

'Come in?' said Joe. 'Help your blooming self!'

He ran upstairs, grabbed his Knockout and down again. Treacle Walker was sitting in the chimney, looking into the stack.

'What ails you, Joseph Coppock?' he said. 'What is wrong?'

'Wrong? Me? There's nowt wrong with me! It's this!' He threw the Knockout into Treacle Walker's lap and sat down on the other side of the fire. 'That's what!'

Treacle Walker turned the pages of the comic. 'It has humour,' he said. 'A nice wit. Charming vernacular. Ah.' He was reading Stonehenge Kit.

'Why's the house there? Why?' said Joe. 'It's a story! Knockout! A story! And it says find out next week! But next week's missing!'

'Has it been written yet?' said Treacle Walker. 'And who is in the window?'

'It's only a comic!'

'"Only"? The house is here, where we sit,' said Treacle Walker. 'And the house is there, where we read, is it not? What is out is in. What is in is out.'

'That's what he said!'

'Who?'

'Him down yonder, in the bog! He said it, too! Before you came!'

'Thin Amren awake still? Thin Amren sleeps.'

'Not now, he doesn't,' said Joe. 'I was talking to him just the other minute. And he said that, same as you: "What's out is in. What's in is out." He did.'

'Thin Amren knows much,' said Treacle Walker.

'Well he doesn't reckon much on you.'

'Alackaday.'

'He knows about that bone thingy of yours. And this.'

Joe went to his museum and took out the jar.

'Yes,' said Treacle Walker. 'Many do.'

'What is it?' said Joe. 'All the Poor Mans Friend and Bridport? What's that about?'

'Beach, Barnicott, Roberts, Bridport? They are foils for those that seek yet are not worthy to achieve. As you may be.'

'I'm only asking what's it for,' said Joe.

'That is the question few have asked,' said Treacle Walker.

'Why? And what's it doing here?'

'You chose it.'

'I liked it. That's all.'

'It held the glamourie.'

'The mucky stuff?' He turned the jar. 'It's gone! There's none left!'

'You saw. You touched. You have. Is that not enough?'

'If it'd fix my wonky eye, I'd be seeing everything same road round; not all sorts.'

'Would you forgo the gift of both?'

'Call that a present?' said Joe. 'I'm neither one nor t'other with it.'

'Or are you more?'

'Lay off.' Joe slumped on the chimney sill. 'I'm fit to skrike.'

XI

'Consider the Bonacon,' said Treacle Walker.

'What's that?' said Joe.

'The creature that passes by at the highmost of the sun.'

'You mean Noony? She's an engine; a train. It's how I tell the time.'

'How does a train, an engine, go?'

'On wheels, of course. How the heck else?'

'And how do the wheels run?'

'On rails.'

'My cart has wheels,' said Treacle Walker. 'It runs by crinkum-crankums, crooks and straights. Yet if I were to set it upon rails, as Bonacon, it would be by straights alone, or off the causeway into the ditch.'

'Noony's got a doings on the side of her wheels to keep her on the rails,' said Joe. 'Your cart hasn't.'

'The doings holds. It turns, yet does not move,' said Treacle Walker. 'Bonacon needs both, for without the one the other is lost. Am I right?'

'Oh, you and your mithering. Give over.'

'Iron Bonacon or wooden cart?' said Treacle Walker. 'Which is the merrier ride? And tell me. Whither and whence the Bonacon? Where does it go to? Where is it come from?'

'I dunno. It just – goes.'

'And at each noon it travels the same path.'

'Yes.'

'How does it return?'

'I've never thought,' said Joe.

'Does it run nidgetwise, as the sun?'

'Search me.'

'And do other Bonacons pass by, in either way?'

'No. Else I couldn't tell the time, could I?'

'And what is your time?'

'When Noony comes I know it's now.'

'"Now"? How can there be Now?'

'That's a daft question,' said Joe.

'But is it?' said Treacle Walker. 'For at the very moment you have Now, it flees. It is gone. It is, on the instant, Then. Surely.'

'You make no sense,' said Joe.

'Bonacon sees where Bonacon is and will be, and knows where it has been. And that is all. You, you know the moment and tell the time. But that is the doings, not the travel; not the wonder, not the sight.'

'Lay off. I said.'

'You ask for help. I give it.'

'You bloody don't!'

'Then be the doings, Joseph Coppock. And let crinkum-crankums run their ways.'

'Oh, forget it,' said Joe. 'What about you? Why are you here? Where are you from?'

'Here on this Middle-Yard is good moundland enough,' said Treacle Walker. 'But my home is the Country of the Summer Stars.'

'Why've you come? What do you want?'

'Ragbone,' said Treacle Walker. 'That is my trade.'

At the door, the iron ring grated, the latch lifted, and the door opened. There was a footstep in the house.

XII

'Now where's he gone?' Joe dreamt he was dreaming and he knew he was.

He opened the door and crossed the white step into the yard. The sun scudded from clouds and the wind was gentle. He went to the pear tree and sat in its shade. He looked up into the branches. The blossom had dropped long since. The pears were small and it was too early for wasps to be about.

He looked through the gateway, across the top of Big Meadow. The alders along the brook were burnished in the light. He saw the copse below.

Joe drowsed in his dream. There was the leaf smell of young poppies. Later the flowers grew tall everywhere all over, bright and different colours, for the one day before petal fall and the green of the heads then the brown rustle of seeds.

He looked down at the slope to the gate. There

were marks in the ground; hoof marks; silver on the grass and cobbles. He stood up. The line of them went to the gate. Joe followed into the field, stepping on each silver hoof. The hooves turned at the hedge and out across the top of Big Meadow onto House Field and down to the brook. They went towards the railway and the tunnel to Common Dean. Joe followed.

The tunnel was high and dark. The hoof marks glowed on bare earth. The arch of the far end showed. Noony rattled by overhead, and the tunnel boomed.

Brambles hung in a curtain from the embankment. He pushed his way through the sharp strands and came out into Common Dean. It was moonlight. The path passed flooded marl pits on either side among alders. The hoof marks were brighter. He followed them between the waters.

They went into Rough Hollow and crossed the brook by a plank bridge to Well Meadow, up into Big Sand Field and Little Sand Field to Round Meadow. Round Meadow was three-sided, and in it was a hillock. And at the foot of the hillock the hoof marks stopped.

Joe walked about the hillock, thinking to himself what it might be. Then he went and sat on its top and looked over the land in the moonlight. And as he sat, beneath him, under the ground, there was music. A pipe played. It was a tune he had never heard, yet he knew it. It played on bone.

'You!'

His shout woke him. He woke from the drowse of the dream in the dream. He was not in his bed on the cupboard by the chimney but at the hillock in Round Meadow. The sun was bright. And the hooves were lost.

'Wait! Wait for us! Wait! Wait! Wait on!'

Nothing. No one. Only loss.

Joe went about the hillock again. It was all smooth turf. He climbed to the top. There was nobody.

He went back down, by Little Sand Field and Big Sand Field, Well Meadow, over the plank bridge into Rough Meadow to Common Dean, along the path between the marl pits' black and flat waters without life.

He parted the brambles at the tunnel and walked on the bare earth. Noony rattled overhead and the tunnel boomed.

Then he went up House Field, along Big Meadow and into the yard.

The white pony and the cart were under the pear tree. Joe ran to them and took hold of the bridle. 'What are you doing? Where is he? Where?' The pony snorted. 'Is he here? Has he come? He must have.' The pony whisked its tail and put its head down to graze. It shook its ears against flies. 'I bet he is. Inside. Cheeky beggar. He knows he should've asked first. It's that chimney. That chimney. He can't get enough of it.'

Joe set off across the yard towards the house. Down in the alder bog a cuckoo called. He reached the door. Inside he heard Treacle Walker's voice, but he could not catch what he was saying.

Joe turned the handle, lifted the latch, and opened the door. He crossed the step.

Treacle Walker was sitting in the chimney, and there was someone else there, opposite, but until he was further into the room Joe could not see who it was. And then he could. It was himself.

XIII

Both Joes yelled. Treacle Walker moved from the sill and put himself between them.

'Stand apart.'

He gripped one in each hand by the neck, his arms wide, and hefted them into the chimney. From the alders a cuckoo called, over and over.

Cuckoo. Cuckoo. Cuckoo. Cuckoo. Cuckoo. Cuckoo. Cuckoo.

He sat the two of them across from each other with the fire basket between.

'Do not touch. Do not speak. Do not look in the eyes.'

He took the bone from his bag, and he played.

It was a tune with wings, trampling things, tightened strings, boggarts and bogles and brags on their feet; the man in the oak, sickness and fever, that set in long, lasting sleep the whole great world with the sweetness of sound the bone did play.

'What the heck was all that about?' said Joe. He swung his feet round on the settle, put his head in his hands.

'Tell me,' said Treacle Walker.

'I can't –'

'Tell me.'

'I – can't.'

'Tell me.'

'I'm – asleep,' said Joe. 'And I'm dreaming. I know I am. There's hoof prints in the yard. Silver. All silver. I follow them. Through the tunnel. To Common Dean. It's moonlight of a sudden. I follow them. Every step. To Round Meadow. Then they go. I can't see them. Then I hear you playing that bone thingy. Under the ground. It wakes me. But I'm not in bed. I'm at Round Meadow still. And it's day. I come back. You're sat in the chimney. We've been talking. About Noony. And a doings. And Stonehenge Kit. And Knockout. And this house. You, going on about ragbone and stars.

Then door opens. And it's me. Stood there and sat in chimney. There's two of us. Him and me. The same. And I'm frit. More than I've ever been. Then there's two of you. Catching hold. One on either side. Then I hear cuckoo. Then you're playing thingy again. I'm being dollied and mangled. Then I'm on the settle. I've got a sick headache. Where's Whizzy?'

'Come to the chimney,' said Treacle Walker. He sat back on the sill and picked up the Knockout.

'Why?' said Joe.

'It is better.'

Joe got up from the settle and went to sit opposite Treacle Walker.

Treacle Walker reached into his bag and took something and put it by him on the sill.

'What have you got in there?' said Joe.

'My little Corr Bolg?' said Treacle Walker. 'This and that. The other and which. Now consider yet again.' He opened the Knockout. 'I hold in my hand a semblance of the house, where Whizzy is depicted. But we are in the actual house, in the chimney, looking at that semblance. And here there is no Whizzy.'

'So we're all right,' said Joe.

'Are we?' said Treacle Walker.

'He can't get in,' said Joe. 'The Brit Basher can't cross the step. I stoned it. See.'

'There, in the semblance, he cannot,' said Treacle Walker. 'Where did you first meet him?'

'He came down a pole with Whizzy. On to my bed. Then they were in the room, chasing Kit. He'd run into the mirror, and they went after him.'

'Into the looking-glass?'

'Yes.'

'Did the glass not break?'

'No. I felt it. After. It's hard.'

'Yet they passed through.'

'Somehow.'

'Some how,' said Treacle Walker. 'Some how. Joseph Coppock. What was in is out. And what was out is in.'

'I stoned the step! You told me to!'

'I did,' said Treacle Walker. 'They cannot cross. Either way. Therefore if they were to come from the glass the step would bar them.'

'But in Knockout they can't get in.'

'And here, where the glass is, they cannot leave. There is the crux.'

'So what must we do?' said Joe.

'"We"? The burden is yours.'

'Why me?'

'It is you that dreams.'

'I'm not dreaming! I'm awake! I am!'

'How do you know that?'

'I do know! I knew I was dreaming when I went to Round Meadow!'

'And then you woke. And where were you but in your dream?'

'You're set on flummoxing me!'

'And if I am not?'

'You are! You! You! You big soft Nelly!'

'That is an appellation new to me,' said Treacle Walker. 'How may it be construed?'

'Sod off!'

Treacle Walker stood and ducked under the mantel beam.

'Where are you going?' said Joe.

'To observe the imperative,' said Treacle Walker. 'If I may.' He went to the door and out into the yard.

'Hang on!'

Treacle Walker sat at the front corner of the cart and took up the reins. Joe ran to him.

'I didn't mean it.' He held the bridle. 'Don't leave us.'

'Come up, then, Joseph Coppock.'

Joe climbed onto the cart and sat next to Treacle Walker.

'Can I have a go?'

'Do as you will.'

Joe took the reins.

'What's her name?'

'She has no name,' said Treacle Walker.

'Why not?'

'She has no need.'

'That's daft.' Joe slapped the reins. 'Gee up!'

The pony put its head down to graze.

'Gee up!'

It flicked its ears again.

'Gee up! Gee up!'

The pony did not even look.

'What's to do with her?'

'Nothing,' said Treacle Walker.

'Then why won't she shift?'

'You do not have the Words.'

'What words?'

'The Words that give you leave.'

'What "leave"?'

'To command,' said Treacle Walker.

'What are they?'

'Who knows?'

'Oh, we're on that game, are we?' said Joe. 'Well, I'm not playing.'

'As you wish,' said Treacle Walker.

Joe dropped the reins and looked behind him.

'You've still got that box.'

'True,' said Treacle Walker.

'Can I have another see at it?'

'You may.'

Joe went to the back of the cart.

'It's not the same.'

'How is it not?' said Treacle Walker.

'There's no name on the plate,' said Joe. 'There's no nothing.'

'Why should it hold a name?' said Treacle Walker.

'I saw it. It was my name.'

Joe lifted the lid. The chest was empty.

'There's nowt there! Where've they gone?'

'Where have what gone?' said Treacle Walker.

'All them jugs and plates.'

'There was one,' said Treacle Walker. 'You took it.'

'There was lots! It was full!'

'They were shimmerings. You chose the true.'

'I don't get you,' said Joe.

'A rainbow is not the light.'

'I could have taken summat else.'

'And you would have held nothing.'

'Flipping heck.' Joe shut the lid.

'There are more matters than philosophy,' said Treacle Walker. 'Go down. I'm to my sod.'

Joe climbed off the cart and stood in the yard. Treacle Walker took the reins, and the pony lifted its head and walked to the gate.

'Then what about my jamas? What did you want them for?'

The pony turned along Big Meadow.

'They are against the day,' said Treacle Walker from beyond the hedge.

'And the lamb!'

'Delectable.'

XIV

'Against the day'? What day?

Joe went back to the house and shut the door.

He's left summat.

On the sill of the chimney, next to where Treacle Walker had been sitting, were Joe's old pyjamas, folded, and a rolled-up comic.

He lifted the pyjamas, and put them down again. The smell, even his own, was too much, and there was another, sickly sour, like the inside of Treacle Walker's coat.

He took the comic to the other side of the fire basket and opened it. It was a Knockout he had not read.

He saw Kiddo the Boy King, and Daffy the Cowboy 'Tec, and Handy Andy the Odd Job Man, and Deed-a-Day Danny, and Daddy Dolittle; and Our Ernie came home and said **WHAT'S FOR TEA,**

MA? and his Pa said DAFT, I CALL IT. and Charlie the caterpillar said IT IS AND ALL. Then he turned the page to Stonehenge Kit the Ancient Brit. At the side was OO-ER, CHUMS. WHIZZY'S LOOSE. HOW WILL OUR HERO GET OUT OF THIS ONE? But the story squares for the pictures were all empty, blank, nothing inside.

He looked at the rest of the comic. Everything else was there.

What the heck?

Joe put the Knockout down.

But I'll reckon him up. Rump and stump, I shall. Rump and stump. I shall that.

Joe went upstairs and stood in front of the mirror.

He felt the glass. It was smooth, without flaw. He could see himself and the room, the cupboard and his bed, the chimney and the door beside, the window and the sky. He went round to the back. It was one piece of black, hard wood; no nails, no screws. He went to the front. The glass had no framing. There were no sides, nowhere that joined, nothing that could be prised apart.

Joe ran downstairs. He took his knife and hacked and snapped and tugged a branch from the pear tree and levered a granite cobble from the paving of the yard and carried it up to the room in both hands. He stood a step away from the glass and held the cobble above his head.

'Right! Cop this, you great nowt!'

With all his strength Joe threw the cobble at the glass.

It hit, and dropped to the floor. The glass did not break. The mirror sang.

He still had the pebbles in his pockets. He took his catapult, put a pebble in the leather pouch, drew back the elastic and fired. The pebble skipped and whined off the glint. He took another. He fired harder. And harder. And harder, harder, harder.

Then there were no pebbles left. His wrists ached and were unsteady. His thumbs had no feeling.

He took his marbles and shot them, faster and faster, even his blood alley, until the floor ran with marbles and pebbles. The mirror was unmarked.

He had only his dobber, the biggest alley with the coloured fire twisting inside. But he could not. Not the dobber.

He put the dobber and his catapult in his pocket and felt for the donkey stone. The roughness was firm on his palm. He weighed the balance, gripped, and smashed the donkey stone onto the glass.

There was no sound. His hand went into the mirror, and the blow dragged him after. He flowed through the mirror. The cold of the passing was none he had ever known.

He stumbled onto the floor of the room. He turned to the mirror. The mirror was not there; only a box of darkness, without surface, without depth. The chimney was in front of him; the door to one side; the cupboard and his bed on the other; the window; but all were the wrong way about. He went to the window.

There was the yard; and the valley; but the gate was to the right, not the left; and so were Barn Croft and Pool Field and Big Meadow and the track. And the track bent the wrong way down to the brook and up to the heath.

He looked back into the room. There was a mirror in the corner.

XV

Joe went into the next room. It was the wrong way. And the stairs turned wrong.

He went down to the chimney. Again the same, with the folded pyjamas and the Knockout on the other side of the fire basket. He looked at the Knockout. The letters and pictures were back to front. And the squares for Stonehenge Kit were blank.

Joe searched the house. It was empty. He opened the door hung wrong and looked across the wrong way yard. The step shone white. He shut the door and went upstairs again.

He stood before the mirror. The reflection showed the room as it should be. He lifted the donkey stone and held it at the glass and pressed gently. The donkey stone passed through, and he saw it and his hand on the other side, as if they had gone into the water of the brook. The cold clamped him.

Joe took a breath and slipped into the room. From the big window the yard and the fields were in their proper place. And there was the same box of dark, and in the corner a mirror.

He went down to the chimney and searched again. Nobody. But the letters of the Knockout were right. He went back to the room and the mirror.

He pressed the donkey stone to the glass and followed it. The cold made him shout, but he ran across the floor and into the next mirror; and on and on, glass after glass, and the rooms flickered and switched with each passing, and the cold grew worse. He went through eight rooms, but in the ninth the cold made him pause for the pain of his breath. He stood, gasping, before the mirror. The room was the right way, and there was banging in his ears.

He lifted his hand to go on. And stopped. The opposite hand in the mirror had not moved to match; the other had. He pressed the stone against the glass, but it was the other hand that had the donkey stone, and they did not meet. And the room reflected was the same as the one he was in.

He changed hands with the donkey stone. The other did the same. He could not get them to meet. He tapped the stone on the glass. The glass was hard.

He pulled back and hit. The glass shattered, and he was looking at emptiness. There was no further to go.

And the banging was not in his head. It was in the cupboard below his mattress. The door quivered under blows and the wood had splintered.

PSST!

He saw the letters in a bubble come from his blankets, and then a face bobbed out. It was Stonehenge Kit.

Kit threw off the blankets and jumped down.

THIS WAY, CHUM!

Kit pointed to the box of dark.

QUICK!

He grabbed Joe's hand. Joe felt a sharp papery grip as he was dragged into the black.

He was running in a tunnel, pulled by a hand he could not see; a black tunnel, turning and lined with stars, so that he could not tell up from down; only the turning; but he ran.

Then light. He was in the room, but a wrong way room, and Kit was holding and running to the next dark.

Again the tunnel, the turning, the stars; and the room; but a right one. Kit let go of his hand and grinned.

FETCH KNOCKOUT AND JAMAS. DON'T DALLY.

Joe ran to the stairs, nearly falling, and to the chimney. He lifted the Knockout and the pyjamas and scrambled back to Kit. Kit took the pyjamas.

Kit said WHIZZY THOUGHT HE HAD US IN THE CUPBOARD, BUT I WAS ON TOP AND SHUT 'EM IN. THEY'LL BE THROUGH IN A JIFF. TAKE KNOCKOUT AND DO A BUNK.

'Where?'

WHEN YOU SEE US, COP US. EH UP! THEY'RE OUT!

Kit took Joe's hand.

RUN, CHUM!

He swung him into the next dark.

Joe was alone in the tunnel, running with the Knockout among the stars, turning, turning, back through flickering rooms, always turning; and he tripped.

He was on his knees, on a floor with pebbles and marbles and granite.

He looked up. In front of him was the chimney. He saw the doorway; he saw the cupboard. There was no box of dark. It was his own room. The Knockout was in his hand.

Joe got to his feet. He was standing in front of the mirror, but he did not see himself. He saw a nest of mirrors, going back and back, and in them Kit was running towards him, and behind were Whizzy and the Brit Basher. The Brit Basher caught up with Kit and lifted his club; but Kit dropped the pyjamas and ran on.

The Brit Basher said **GOTCHA!** And he started to wallop the pyjamas **BIFF! BAM! THWACK!**

OAF! LUMMOX! AND CLOD! THAT'S NOT HIM! said Whizzy.

IT IS, GUV! SNIFF THE WHIFF!

And the Brit Basher went on walloping the pyjamas. Of course, this let Kit off, and he ran.

He ran through mirrors and mirrors, growing bigger, getting nearer, until he was one mirror away and the Brit Basher and Whizzy were catching up right behind him. And Kit shouted **KNOCKOUT!**

Joe opened the Knockout and pressed it to the glass.

He felt the paper squirm under his palms. He leaned with all his force. The paper writhed, twitched. He kept his weight against the glass until pain made him drop the comic. He looked in the mirror and saw himself.

The Knockout lay splayed on the floor. He picked it up. It was open at the squares of Stonehenge Kit; but the squares were not empty. In the first was the room with the cupboard and the chimney. The cupboard door was smashed and Whizzy and the Brit Basher were coming out. Whizzy said **AFTER**

'EM! BIFF HIM FOR THAT BRICK! AND GET THAT POT HE'S GOT!

The next picture was Kit running through a wrong way room and being chased by Whizzy and the Brit Basher,

Next was Kit with his thumbs in his ears, wiggling his fingers and saying **HA HA HA! HEE HEE HEE! CAN'T CATCH ME FOR A PENNY CUP OF TEA!**

Next was a right way room, and Kit was opening the big window.

Next he was climbing out of the window, and the next he was swinging on a gutter and reaching for a drainpipe.

Next he was shinning down the drainpipe into the yard.

Next he was running across the yard and Whizzy was leaning out of the window and saying **FUME! AND BAH!**

Next Whizzy was on the drainpipe and the Brit Basher had his club between his teeth and was reaching for the gutter and Kit was running through the gateway.

Next the Brit Basher had hold of the drainpipe and let go of the gutter; but he was so heavy he pulled the drainpipe off the wall and fell **OOF! ZONK! KER-POW! SPLAT!** on Whizzy, and Kit was running down the track between Big Meadow and Barn Croft. And at the side it said **PHEW! THAT WAS CLOSE! BUT WHIZZY'S OUT OF THE HOUSE AND HE CAN'T GET BACK IN! WHAT WILL HAPPEN NEXT, CHUMS?**

XVI

Joe went down to the well and pumped a bucket of water and carried it back up to his room and stood before the mirror. He dipped the donkey stone in the bucket and held it to the glass. But before it touched he stopped.

He pulled out his handkerchief and sloshed it in the water and rubbed it on the donkey stone until the handkerchief was covered in grey. Then he rubbed the handkerchief lightly over the glass, not pressing, down and up and round and across, until none of the glass showed and there was only a panel of grit.

He rinsed the handkerchief, took the bucket downstairs and emptied it onto the yard.

'And that,' said Joe, 'is that.'

XVII

'Would that it were,' said Treacle Walker.

He was under the pear tree. The pony grazed.

'What the heck!' said Joe. 'Just when I've got things straight, you have to turn up like a bad penny!'

'Wae's me,' said Treacle Walker. 'Yet I am no coin of Luxembourg.' He went towards the house. Joe followed.

Treacle Walker stood at the step. 'May I pass?'

'Don't be daft. Course you can.'

Treacle Walker went to the chimney and sat on the sill. Joe ran upstairs and fetched the Knockout. He handed it to Treacle Walker.

'See? Everything's right now.'

'That is done,' said Treacle Walker.

'Yes. It is.'

'Done; but not over.'

'Oh, give it a rest,' said Joe. 'I've had enough.'

'Indeed?'

'Yes, I blooming well have. Look. Whizzy and them are back in Knockout. I did what you said. What more do you want?'

'I? Nothing.'

'Then we're quits.'

Treacle Walker did not answer. Joe stared at the ashes of the fire.

'Treacle Walker.'

'Joseph Coppock.'

'You say you make people better.'

'I heal all things; save jealousy.'

'Can you make me better?'

'Are you not well?'

'Can you make my eyes proper?'

'"Proper"?'

'I can't tell what's real and what isn't.'

'What is "real", Joseph Coppock?'

'Don't start that.'

'You chose the glamourie.'

'I never.'

'But you did choose. The choice was yours. You could have chosen shimmerings. You did not.'

'How was I to know? Anyroad, what use is it?'

'I can give you back your blindness,' said Treacle Walker. 'Be a doings, if you will.'

Joe stared at the ashes. For a moment his name glowed silver embers.

XVIII

'Come up, Joseph Coppock,' said Treacle Walker. 'It is time to make an end.'

'End of what?' said Joe.

'Of what you began.'

'Me? I never began nowt.'

'Bring your knife, the stone, the dobber and Poor Mans Friend.'

They left the house and crossed the yard.

'Where are we for?' said Joe.

'Not far.'

Treacle Walker went into Big Meadow and down to the bog. He stopped at the bank.

'Take an alder young enough for your knife and cut five green branches the length of your arm, and bring them here.'

'Why?'

'Do it.'

'Show us how.'

'I will not enter.'

'I need my wellies,' said Joe.

'Go,' said Treacle Walker. 'And cover the eye, lest you be lost.'

'He told me not to. I mustn't use my patch. He said.'

'I tell you. Go.'

'It's sopping wet in there. I'll be back in a sec.'

'Go.'

'You're in a right bate, you are.'

Joe took out his patch, put it over his good eye, and stepped onto the bog.

At first there were tussocks of grass, but soon everywhere was the water, slutch and roots. He sank to his shins, each step a heave and suck.

He found a sapling in a clear space, with branches he could reach and hack.

'How many?'

'Five.'

'Why?'

'They are enough.'

Joe cut five green branches.

'Will these do?'

'They must,' said Treacle Walker.

Joe worked his way back to the bank. 'I'm soaked. Them midges are killing me.'

'Strip the branches,' said Treacle Walker.

Joe lopped off the spurs and leaves.

'Make sharp the ends,' said Treacle Walker.

Joe whittled the wood to a point. The sap turned red.

'Lay them on the bank, and stand by me.'

Joe put the branches down, stepped over the bank and stood next to Treacle Walker.

Treacle Walker spoke into the bog. 'Thin Amren. Thin Amren. Come from the mools. I want thee.'

He waited. Only the wings of insects could be heard.

Treacle Walker spoke again. 'Thin Amren. Thin Amren. Come from the mools. I want thee.'

The sound of a wind stirred; but the leaves of the alders were quiet, and Joe felt no wind on his face.

'Thin Amren. Thin Amren. Come from the mools. I want thee.'

The sound of wind grew louder, but Joe felt nothing. Then the air and the whole land trembled. The alder trunks rippled as rope, and the bog heaved without moving. Joe grabbed Treacle Walker's coat.

'Are you here, Treacle Walker?' The voice was in the trees.

'I am here,' said Treacle Walker.

'And why are you here?'

'You know what must be,' said Treacle Walker.

'And what must be?' The voice was all around.

'Thin Amren sleeps.'

'And if he will not?'

'There is no dreaming.'

The sky was a blare of sick headache.

'I do not dream.'

'Joseph Coppock,' said Treacle Walker. 'Move the patch. You have cause for all glamourie.'

Joe swivelled the patch across to cover his weak eye. The bog opened before him further than he could tell.

Treacle Walker spoke. 'Thin Amren, why do you not sleep?'

'I am alone.'

'What do you lack?'

'Whirligig.'

'He is mine,' said Treacle Walker. 'As I am his.'

'I laugh with Whirligig,' said the voice. 'Laugh truly. Give me Whirligig.'

'It cannot be.'

'Till I have Whirligig, I will not sleep.'

'Then cuckoo shall rule over nothingness.'

'Let cuckoo rule. I will not dream.'

The bog was silent.

Joe clutched the coat more. 'What's he on about? Whirligig. Cuckoo. Dream. What's he on at?'

'Thin Amren dreams all that is and is not,' said Treacle Walker. 'He dreams Thin Amren. We are his dreams.'

The alders swung and the land lurched. Above the house, the sky cracked. And in the crack was a claw. The claw rent down, and the gap was blackness moving, mirror cold, with snow.

'Hold fast,' said Treacle Walker. 'This is no hurlothrumbo. No lomperhomock, this. This is Winter. This is Night.'

Again the sky was torn. And in the gap was a bird; huge, wings spread, claws open to clench the house. Cuckoo. Cuckoo. Cuckoo. Cuckoo. Cuckoo. Cuckoo. Cuckoo. Cuckoo. Cuckoo. Cuckoo. Cuckoo.

The blackness surged. It flowed from the sky, across the embankment, into the yard. It seethed up the house, the roof, the walls, the windows and the door. It was an ivy of black climbing the pear tree. It bulged against the hedge and spilled out onto Big Meadow and down the field towards Treacle Walker and Joe.

And thunder with no pause. Joe shut his eye against the lightnings and the dark.

Across the purple swirl on his lids, he saw a bubble, and in the bubble **DOBBER NOW ELSE WHIZZY WINS! T'RA, JOE!**

Cuckoo. Cuckoo. Cuckoo. Cuckoo. Cuckoo. Cuckoo. Cuckoo. Cuckoo. Cuckoo. Cuckoo. Cuckoo. Cuckoo. Cuckoo.

Joe opened his eye and fumbled in his pocket for his catapult and dobber. He put the dobber in the pouch, drew, and shot without aim. The dobber flew straight and hit the bird square on the breast. There was a flash that was not from thunder, and the bird went up in a flame of fire. It devoured the dark, burnt the blackness. It cleansed house, pear, yard, field, land and air with light, and blinded Joe. But when his eye cleared, the bird, night, and thunder were gone.

'Stone the sky,' said Treacle Walker.

Joe took the donkey stone and dipped it in the waters of the bog and reached up to the sky and rubbed. He drew the gaps together with the stone and closed them, smooth, without seam. But still the trees rippled and the ground quaked.

'Go to him,' said Treacle Walker.

Joe picked up the sharpened branches and went out onto the bog. He passed over the mire without sinking, into the endless copse.

Thin Amren lay by an alder stool. He smiled. 'I dreamed Whirligig would come,' he said. 'I dreamed he would.' He looked older. His limbs were slack, his belly hollowed and swollen, and his bones showed through the skin. 'But I was away from the wet too long, so I was.'

'Course I've come,' said Joe. 'Did you ever think I'd not?'

'I see what Whirligig has fetched.'

'You must sleep,' said Joe. 'You've got to.'

'I'm weary. Weary of dreaming, Whirligig. Whirligig shall stay; and together we shall laugh the sky.'

'We can't.'

'"Can't never did." I tellt at the start. Has that carnaptious coptank snatched Whirligig in his Corr Bolg, then?'

'If you won't dream,' said Joe, 'I can't be. Ever. At all. But if you dream, I can. Happen we'll meet. Happen we'll not. But we'll remember. "Cut my throat and hope to die." We'll not forget.'

'That's the skewer,' said Thin Amren. 'The skewer. So it is. The stab. Yet Whirligig has wisdom on him. He has the wisdom. He has it. Whirligig. Well, well.

What larks. But will he be giving a body a drink? For I'm thirsty dry.'

Joe took the jar and filled it from a clean pool between the roots of the alder and held it to Thin Amren's lips. Thin Amren drank, gulping.

He lay back on the bog.

'What larks, eh? Whirligig?'

'What larks.'

'Thrust me deep and stake me quick.'

Joe cradled Thin Amren and dragged him onto open bog and, both hands flat on his chest, with all his weight he pressed him down. Thin Amren sank into the water. His face showed; then leaves and mud ran over and covered it. Joe could feel him as he pressed. Thin Amren moved, settled, and was still. Joe wept, and, weeping, pressed him further, until Thin Amren was at the end of Joe's reach. Then he took one of the alder branches, felt for Thin Amren's neck, and bent the branch across, and drove the sharp ends into the bog on either side of the flesh. He took another and felt for an arm and pinned it at the elbow. He sobbed and swore with every thrust. Then he took a branch for the other arm; then another and another for the two legs.

His face was slutched, and his tears mingled with leaves and water. He knelt in the mire.

'Thin Amren. Sleep you on.'

Joe stood, lifted his patch, and waded back across the bog. It lost its endlessness and he saw the bank and stepped over to where Treacle Walker was. He could not stop the tears. He fell and held on to Treacle Walker. 'I'm only little. I'm only little.'

Treacle Walker helped Joe up, and they went to the house. Joe nodded when they came to the doorstep. They sat in the chimney, facing each other across the fire basket. Treacle Walker put the Corr Bolg on the floor.

In the middle of the ashes lay a speckled egg.

'It's cuckoo's,' said Joe.

He reached out and lifted the egg. He opened his hand to look. He was holding the dobber, its flames clear in the glass.

'Just like that.'

He brought kindling of oak twigs and holly bark

and laid them in the basket with twists of a scrumpled Knockout under, and lit the fire. The twigs crackled. The holly bark caught, and white billows lifted into the stack. Treacle Walker watched them rise.

They sat and listened to the fire.

'Treacle Walker?'

'Joseph Coppock.'

'I hadn't seen.'

'What had you not seen, Joseph Coppock?'

'It was me. I started it. I fetched cuckoo. With yon thingy. First off.'

'It was the man that sang in the marrow bone.'

'No. It was me. I did it.'

Joe watched the flames, bright as the dobber; listened to them.

'To heck with that caper. To heck with it all.' He put thorn logs on the fire. Sparks climbed in the smoke. 'Eh. Treacle Walker.'

'Joseph Coppock.'

'I know what's the titchiest thing there is. Do you?'

'I do not. What is the titchiest thing there is?'

'A dimple on a pimple on a money spider's knee.'

'A dimple on a pimple on a patella of Linyphia. That would be minuscule, I must allow,' said Treacle Walker.

'And can you tell me this?' said Joe. 'What goes up a chimney down but not down a chimney up?'

'I cannot.'

'It's a riddle,' said Joe.

'For ashes.'

'No. A joke. See?'

'Ah,' said Treacle Walker. 'But alas. What goes up a chimney down though not down a chimney up is beyond my thought. I have no badinage.'

'Guess! Go on!'

'I cannot. I concede.'

'It's an umberella!' said Joe. 'Get it?'

'Joseph Coppock, you are quite the droll.'

'If you open an umberella,' said Joe, 'you can't shove it either road. But if you shut it you can.'

'That is true. Your knowledge eclipses mine.'

They sat.

'You really are daft,' said Joe. He moved the logs. 'Treacle Walker?'

'Joseph Coppock.'

'Treacle Walker, am I dead?'

'I will not say that you are dead. Rather, in this world you have changed your life, and are got into another place.'

Joe watched the flames.

'Fair do's. Treacle Walker?'

'Joseph Coppock.'

'What is it you want for you? What is it you want most? For you. Not some wazzock else.'

'Never has a soul asked that of me.'

'What's the answer?'

Treacle Walker leaned his head against the timber behind him and looked up into the stack.

'To hear no more the beat of Time. To have no morrow and no yesterday. To be free of years.' He closed his eyes. 'Oblivion. Home.'

'That's not daft.'

'It is everything.'

'You're shent,' said Joe. He reached round the fire and picked up the Corr Bolg. 'Come on. Let's be having you.' He took his dobber, the Poor Mans

Friend, the donkey stone from his pocket, laid them together beside the bone, and slung the Corr Bolg about his shoulder. 'Buck up, Treacle Walker.' He bent forward. 'And bugger off to summer stars.'

He freed his patch and dropped it on the fire. It flared and was gone. He left the chimney and opened the door; crossed the shining step. He ran to the pear tree, jumped onto the cart, stood at the front edge. He slapped the reins.

The Words came, to his mouth, to his mind, from within and without and the dark and the light and the knowing. 'Kosko gry! Kosko gry! Muk man kistur tute knaw!'

The pony started from the yard, legs and tail outstretched, head forward, thin, through the gate, down the track, between Big Meadow, Barn Croft and Pool Field, over the brook.

It was midday. The sky shone. Noony rattled past, and her smoke curled along the valley.

'Ragbone! Ragbone! Any rags! Pots for rags! Donkey stone!'